DIGORY

AND THE LOST KING

DIGORY
AND THE LOST KING

ANGELA MCALLISTER

illustrated by Ian Beck

BLOOMSBURY

This edition published in Great Britain in 2006
by Bloomsbury Publishing Plc,
36 Soho Square, London, W1D 3QY
Text copyright © Angela McAllister 2006
Illustrations copyright © Ian Beck 2006
The moral rights of the author and illustrator have been asserted

A CIP record of this book is available from the
British Library

ISBN 0 7475 8483 4
ISBN-13 9780747584834

Printed in Great Britain by Clays Ltd, St Ives plc

10 9 8 7 6 5 4 3 2 1

All papers used by Bloomsbury Publishing are natural, recyclable products
made from wood grown in well-managed forests.
The manufacturing processes conform to the environmental
regulations of the country of origin.

For Archie – A. M.
To Frances Holloway – I. B.

CONTENTS

Chapter One

HOW THINGS TURN OUT

IN days of old, when knights were bold, there lived a boy called Digory. He had lanky legs, ginger hair and a nose like a chipolata.

Digory came from a village called Batty-by-Noodle where nothing much happened – and that's the way he liked it. All Digory wanted was to wander through the forest, poke about in streams, make up songs and play his lute.

However, things don't always turn out the way we'd like. (Have you noticed?)

Somehow Digory had been mistaken for a dragon-slaying hero and had been made a knight.

Somehow he had been sent off on a deaf, old carthorse called Barley to fight dragons and do noble deeds.

Somehow, despite running *away* from dragons, he had managed to do noble deeds anyway and been made a prince by grateful King Widget, who didn't have a prince of his own.

So, in days of old when knights were bold, Prince Digory lived in Widget Castle, with the King, the Queen and his best friend, Princess Enid. And he was just a bit older than you.

An Invitation

It was breakfast time at Widget Castle.

As usual, everything on the table had a label – coddled eggs, marigold pie, plum pudding and dandelion wine. This was to help forgetful King Widget, who had trouble remembering the names of things.

The Queen also had a label, pinned to her robe. (In fact, she had a selection of labels to choose from; 'Her Majesty' for when she was out and about in the realm, 'She Who Must Be Obeyed' for when she was in a bad mood and 'Snugglepumpkin' for when she was alone with the King.)

'Now,' said the Queen as she served everyone a royal-size portion of plum pudding, 'is anything important happening this week?'

'Digory and I are going to make a nest box for owls,' said Enid.

'Oh good,' said the Queen.

'Enid and I are going to put a new roof on our treehouse,' said Digory.

'Oh good,' said the Queen.

'And I've organised a bit of a whatsit,' said the King.

'Oh dear!' The Queen sighed.

'Yes,' said the King, 'we're going to have . . . um . . . oh, you know . . .'

'What *sort* of thing are we going to have?' asked Enid. 'Animal, vegetable or mineral?'

'Animal? Yes, animals – lots of 'em,' said the King happily.

Digory's heart sank. He hoped these animals weren't dragons. Once before the King had sent him on an errand to slay a dragon, which had resulted in a very uncomfortable adventure. (Digory still wasn't sure what had actually happened. He knew he'd tried to trick the dragon, chased it, run away from it, nearly been gobbled up by it, flown on its back, *actually* been gobbled up by it, mysteriously escaped and . . . well . . . somehow the dragon had disappeared.)

Digory was certain that he never wanted to see another dragon ever, ever again.

'Is it a hamster, Your Majesty?' he asked hopefully.

'Hamster! Ha ha!' the King roared with laughter.

'No, no, no, Diggers. It's a . . . a . . . charge and thrust!' He stabbed at the air with an imaginary weapon. 'It's a strike and blow, a bump and tumble!'

Suddenly Enid jumped up and ran out of the breakfast chamber. A moment later she returned carrying a broom.

'I know!' She took up the reins of an imaginary pony, lowered the broomstick and began galloping up and down the room.

'Oh yes!' cried the Queen, clapping her

hands with glee. 'Of course . . . it's a joust! Clever girl.'

'That's it!' The King beamed. Enid dropped the broom and flung her arms around her father. 'Haven't had one for ages. Used to joust with my brother . . . um . . .'

'Wortle,' said the Queen.

'Bless you,' said the King.

'No, Wortle – it's your brother's name. King Wortle.'

'Oh yes, so it is – or at least it *was*,' said the King mysteriously. He heaved a great sigh and a sudden sadness overcame the whole family. They fell silent.

Digory was puzzled. He had never heard of King Wortle before. Why did the mention of his name make everyone so sad?

Before Digory had a chance to ask, Cook arrived with a bowl of plump shiny strawberries, which stirred everyone out of their gloomy mood.

'As I was saying,' muttered the King, helping himself to the fattest fruit, 'Wortle and I

15

always used to get together and organise a bit
of fun-and-games the week before our birthday, Diggers. You know, invite all the village
and the next-door-nosy-nobles round.'

'Daddy and Wortle are twins,' whispered
Enid in Digory's ear.

'But we haven't done it for a while.' A royal
frown crumpled King Widget's brow. The
Queen quickly handed him another straw-
berry. 'Anyway,' the King continued, 'the
birthday's coming up and as we've got Digory
here now, I thought we'd have a . . . whatever
it is . . . broom-bashing.'

'Joust, Daddy, joust!' squealed Enid.

'Just what I was thinking,' said the King. 'Fixed one up for Saturday. Shouldn't be a problem for a young prince like you, Diggers. Too old for it myself these days. Great fun, yes. Charge and thrust, charge and thrust!'

Digory's breakfast turned to stone in his tummy. 'But I don't know how to joust, Your Majesty,' he protested.

'Plenty of time for practice,' said the King. 'It's only Wednesday today. Practice makes perfect, Digory my lad.'

And that was the end of that.

Well, that wasn't the end of that. It was just the beginning for Prince Digory.

PRACTICE MAKES PERFECT

Poor Digory went off to the stables to tell Barley the bad news.

Barley, his deaf, old carthorse, knew as

much about jousting as Digory did. She adopted Digory's unhappy mood and chewed her gums in a what-about-retiring-me-to-a-quiet-meadow? sort of way.

Digory, ignoring her silent plea, sat on an upturned bucket and composed a song called 'I'd rather eat gorse than be knocked off my horse'. That was how Enid found him.

Enid always understood Digory. She was the first true friend he'd ever had. She wasn't huffy and proud like the other princesses Digory had met doing his noble deeds. She didn't sit in a tower all day, combing her long, golden hair. She didn't even *have* long, golden hair – hers was mud brown and stuck up like a hodgepig. She liked to wander through the forest, poke about in streams, climb trees and play her crumhorn. Enid, you see, was an unusual sort of princess and had a lot in common with Digory, who was an unusual sort of knight. Best of all, she always had a smile and a good idea.

'Cheer up,' she said, giving Barley a bite of her apple. 'It won't be so bad, Digory. I'll help you practise for the joust.'

'But I don't want to knock you off your horse with a stick,' sighed Digory. 'I might hurt you. In fact, I don't want to knock anyone off their horse.'

'It's not a stick, it's a lance,' laughed Enid, 'and that's the point of a jousting tournament. You must topple your opponent or he'll topple you first.'

Digory had no doubt at all that he was going to wake up on Sunday morning covered in bumps and bruises.

'Try *pretending* to be fierce and competitive,' said Enid, 'even if you don't feel it. Just start by pretending. You might surprise yourself.'

Digory thought of his bold brothers, Arthur and Tom. They really *were* fierce and competitive. They competed over who could chop firewood the fastest, who could trap the biggest boar, even who could stuff the most crumpets into his mouth at once.

And Digory's sister, Ethelburg, captain of the Mucky Maidens' Mudflinging Team, was fierce and competitive too. No one was fiercer than Ethelburg when her team was losing, as she thundered towards her opponents like a mud tempest, with flashing wild eyes and bloodcurdling shrieks.

Even Digory's mother, Betsy the blacksmith, competed each year in the local hammer-tossing championship and remained unbeaten.

But Digory wasn't like that.

'There's room for all sorts, son,' his Dad used to say. 'Just be yourself.'

But there's only room for one sort at a joust, thought Digory, *and it's definitely the fierce, competitive sort.* Maybe pretending *was* the only way. He looked at Enid's excited face.

'All right, I'll try,' he said with a heavy heart.

'I knew you would!' said Enid, tweaking his nose.

At these words Barley stamped a hoof disapprovingly, as if maybe she wasn't quite so deaf after all . . .

So began Digory's apprenticeship in jousting. For the rest of the week he cantered around the tilting yard on Barley, stabbing a lance at a sack stuffed with straw. Enid never ran out of encouraging words, but by Friday night she had a sore throat from shouting so much and Digory hadn't hit the sack once!

'If only we had more time to train,' croaked Enid. 'It's just a matter of balance and timing . . .'

'And aim and strength, and horsemanship and bravery,' groaned Digory. 'Not much to master in three days! If only it was a sword fight instead.' Digory had been given a magic sword by an unreliable wizard called Burdock. (The magic always took some time to warm up, but the sword had turned out to be jolly useful.)

'That wouldn't be fair,' said Enid.

'I don't think the joust will be fair either,' said Digory. 'Everyone else will be much better than me.'

Even Enid couldn't argue with that. But as we have noticed before, things don't always turn out the way you expect . . .

Time To Pretend

On the morning of the joust King Widget woke up with a terrible case of the sneezes.

'Oh, what a pity,' sighed the Queen, plumping up his pillows. 'I'm afraid you'll have to stay at home.'

'Bodder!' grumbled the King. 'Ah don't want to mith the j . . . j . . . j'atishoo!'

'I shall send for hot soup and hot-water bottles and hankies and jigsaws,' said the Queen. 'Maybe, if you feel a little better this afternoon, you could watch from the battlements. But now I can hear the tent poles being hammered into the green. I'm afraid I must go and make sure Digory has a jolly good break-fast.' And she bustled off to fuss over the cook.

The Queen had ordered up a great feast to start the day. But poor Digory had no appetite. He sat at the breakfast table, staring at his plate. Two fried eggs and a sausage jeered at him with a mocking grin. Digory's tummy turned somersaults and wouldn't settle down, even for a sausage with a doubtful sense of humour.

Enid, however, had been watching the tournament preparations since dawn, and was excited enough to eat for two.

Digory secretly slid his breakfast into his napkin, so as not to disappoint the Queen. Then he slipped away to prepare Barley.

However, at the stable, Digory discovered that the old horse had somehow got wind of the galloping and poking that was soon to take place and had stubbornly turned her back to the door, refusing to budge. It needed four squires and a handful of peppermints to persuade her out.

Meanwhile, guests began to arrive from every corner of the kingdom. Bold knights galloped around the moat, impatient to begin the competition. Damsels tried to distract them by getting into distress all over the place. Flags fluttered, muffin men strolled

among the gaily coloured tents and the village children found plenty of mischief.

Digory put on his cold, clammy armour. It

made him shiver so much his teeth rattled. He remembered how proud his mother Betsy had been the day she made it for him. *She really believed I was brave enough to slay a dragon*, he thought as he pulled on his gauntlets.

Then Digory looked at Enid, who had come to give his tin boots one last polish. She believed he was brave too – brave enough to joust for the King. And curiously, as he considered this, Digory's teeth stopped rattling and he warmed up a little inside. (For I expect you know that when someone believes in you, your heart swells like a sun-ripe peach. And that's bound to warm you up a bit, isn't it?)

When all the straps were strapped and the buckles buckled, Digory was hoisted on to Barley's back. Enid gave the old carthorse a good-luck carrot.

'Remember,' she whispered to Digory as she handed him his lance and shield, 'remember to pretend . . .'

Chapter Two

THE NEVER-ENDING JOUST

As Digory plodded out into the sunshine the sweet smell of muffins hit his nose and the local villagers began to cheer. With this encouragement he tried a fierce and competitive smile. The crowd cheered louder. *This is not so bad*, Digory thought. As usual, Enid was right. Maybe he just had to pretend after all. Digory had often played pretend games on his own before he met Enid. Now he imagined he was the fearless champion of the joust. He stuck out his chin, as proud knights do, and waved his gauntlet boldly. The crowd whistled and clapped.

But the champion's smile soon faded from Digory's face when he turned the corner and saw the other knights and princes, assembled together. *They were all huge, they were all bold and they were all obviously fearless! (And what a collection of very proud chins!)*

Now, to add to his sudden terror, Digory was told that he was to go last. Poor Digory had to wait and watch the rest of the knights pulverise each other. Knocked sideways, armour crumpled and bones broken, they fell to the ground, groaning, and were carried away to the first-aid tent.

As the last pair of knights trotted forward to tilt their lances to the Queen, Digory bent down and whispered in Barley's ear. 'I think I'll pretend to be someone else now, someone who lives in the next kingdom . . .' And he gently pulled her reins to lead her quietly away.

But Digory had the unusual habit of always arriving at the place he was trying to avoid. As he and Barley emerged from the maze of tall tents, a great cheer erupted and there they were – facing the crowd.

'Hurray for Prince Digory!' yelled the local villagers.

'Digory for champion!'

A ploughman's boy ran up and tied a ribbon on to Barley's rein and the Queen smiled down from her garden throne nearby and said, 'Good luck, Digory, dear. Remember what the King said – charge and thrust.'

Enid, sitting beside her mother, screwed up her face and made a fierce expression. Digory understood. He summoned all his pretending-power to feel like a jousting champion, but he could only feel like a quivering jelly.

'Oh well, Barley,' he said. 'Here we go.'

Digory pulled down his visor. Inside the dark helmet he suddenly had one last, desperate hope. Maybe he would wake up and find it was just a terrible dream after all . . .

THE FEARSOME FOE . . .

But Digory didn't wake up.

Drums rolled. The crowd hushed.

'Step forward, Prince Digory of Widget Castle,' bellowed the local butcher, who was announcing things, 'and Lord Percy of Rosebud Manor.'

At the other end of the field Digory's opponent stepped forward. To Digory's amazement, Lord Percy was small and thin. Even his armour had knobbly knees. His horse, which looked suspiciously like a pony, was old and tatty. Digory guessed that both horse and rider knew as little about jousting as he and Barley did.

For once Digory was right.

With a fanfare of trumpets the joust began.

Lord Percy's horse strolled over to the nearest flag and began to eat it.

Barley sat down.

Lord Percy dismounted and tugged his horse back to the start.

Digory dismounted and gave Barley a big nudge.

Lord Percy and Digory, in their heavy armour, had to be hoisted on to their chargers all over again.

Lord Percy lowered his lance and promptly fell off.

Digory lowered his lance and got it tangled up in his reins. Then he fell off.

The crowd collapsed in fits of laughter. It seemed Digory *had* been fairly matched after all.

The joust continued like this for three hours. Lord Percy broke four lances, two pairs of reins and charged into the first-aid tent, scattering spectators over the nearest hedge.

Digory broke three lances, lost a tin boot and snagged the royal tent ropes, bringing the whole tent down like a parasol.

The Queen and her guests recovered while the tent was put up again. Then the combat had to go on because there was still no winner – and the rules of the tournament said there had to be a winner, one way or another.

'Let the combat proceed,' bellowed the butcher. 'Now with swords!'

'No. I don't think that's wise,' said the Queen. 'Let's go straight to fisticuffs.'

'Fisticuffs!' yelled the butcher.

Digory hadn't practised this. But neither, it seemed, had Lord Percy.

Lord Percy swiped out and hit himself on the chin.

Digory walloped Lord Percy, who ducked, and hit himself on the head.

Lord Percy dodged about like a flitting but-
terfly, stepped back and fell over his exhaust-
ed horse.

Digory ran forward, fists waving madly in
the air, and tripped over his own lost boot.

And so the fisticuffs match went on – for
two hours.

AT LAST . . .

At last a cart carrying a small barrel was
wheeled up.

Thank goodness, thought Digory, who was
hot and thirsty, *a barrel of water*.

'Conkers!' bawled the butcher and he threw
Digory and Lord Percy a ball of string. Sure
enough the barrel was full of conkers of all
shapes and sizes, helpfully drilled with holes.

Digory's heart sank.

Lord Percy's heart sank.

But there had to be a winner.

Digory and Lord Percy chose their conkers
and threaded them on to strings.

Once more they faced each other.

Once more the crowd held its breath. (Well,
the parts of the crowd that hadn't given up
and gone home. The parts of the crowd still
left that hadn't gone to sleep.)

Lord Percy bent forward and whispered.

'Shall we run away? There's maypole dancing today in the next kingdom.'

Digory thought for a moment: *Maypole dancing, music, toffee apples, sitting on a grassy bank, watching the fair . . . What a great idea.* Then he saw Enid, still making fierce, competitive faces to spur him on.

'No,' sighed Digory, not quite able to hide his regret. For Enid's sake he attempted a fearful scowl. 'Raise your conker, you . . . you stinker!'

Thwack! Lord Percy swung his conker and it whizzed off its string, hurtled straight through the castle window, bounced off the kitchen wall and plopped into the cooking pot, splashing cook with custard.

'Oh dear,' sighed the Queen with a yawn, 'something tells me we could be here until bedtime.'

And she was right.

There followed two hours of conker bonking. Conkers flew perilously at the few loyal spectators left. Conkers splashed into the lake, terrifying the swans, and broke every window on that side of the castle. Digory and Lord Percy were dented all over, with fine black eyes each.

Still there was no winner between them.

When a conker landed, bullseye, on the butcher's bald bonce, he decided enough was enough.

'Tiddlywinks!' he bellowed.

'Thank goodness,' sighed the Queen. Now, she knew this was one sport that Digory had practised very well, as the whole family loved to play tiddlywinks by the fire on winter evenings. But, as luck would have it, so did Lord Percy's family too.

Two hours later, Baron Squinteye, who was sitting behind the Queen, leant forward and whispered in her ear.

'Might I mention, Your Majesty, for the future, that tiddlywinks is not much fun to watch.' He peered down at Digory and Lord Percy flipping their tiny counters across an upturned barrel. 'They're so, well they're so *tiddly*!'

But the Queen just muttered 'Fluff 'n' fiddlestuff.' For she too had finally nodded off to sleep.

Snnnrrrrgh . . .

Digory and Lord Percy played tiddlywinks until twilight. Still there was no winner between them.

By the time they had eventually lost the last tiddlywink in the grass, even the butcher had gone home, hoping his greedy family had left a chop for his supper.

'How should we compete now?' asked Digory.

'First one home?' suggested Lord Percy.

'Musical statues!' shouted one of the crowd.

'Loudest bottom burps!' shouted the other one of the crowd.

'Stuffing the most ferrets down your trousers,' said a poacher (busy stuffing as many leftover muffins as he could down his).

'I know,' said Enid wearily, 'what about thumb wrestling?' As this was a sitting-down sort-of sport Digory and Lord Percy agreed. They clamped their fists together.

'Repeat after me,' said Enid. 'One, two, three, four. I declare a thumb war. Stand, bow, fight!'

The thumbs stood, bowed and fought. And for such little chaps it was a furious combat.

Digory had superior strength from playing the lute, but Lord Percy had some nifty moves.

'Hup!'

'Ha!'

'Oi!'

'Ow!'

It was all over in a minute. Lord Percy's

thumb fell, stunned, on to his palm. Digory's delighted digit wiggled triumphantly!

'I've won!' he cried. 'I've won at last!' Digory creaked to his feet and raised his champion thumb to the crowd . . . but no one cheered. The last two spectators had left with the poacher to scoff the muffins and everyone else had fallen asleep or gone home.

Lord Percy, nursing his defeated warrior, stumbled off to his tent, just pleased that it was all over.

Only Enid remained to congratulate Digory. 'Well done,' she said proudly. 'I knew you could do it. Now, let's wake Mummy and all go home to bed.'

At the sound of the word 'bed' Digory yawned happily. How he got there he never remembered.

Chapter Three

LOST KINGS

WHEN the Queen, Enid and Digory returned to the castle after the tournament that evening, the King had already gone to bed.

'Poor dear Widgey,' sighed the Queen. 'An early night will do him good.' She decided not to disturb him and slept in the spare bedchamber instead.

Next morning everyone had a jolly good lie-in. In fact, nobody got up for breakfast at all. It wasn't until the smell of roast chicken wafted up the spiral staircase that the Queen, Enid and Digory got up for lunch.

'I hope the King remembered to have some supper last night,' fretted the Queen. 'His forgetfulness has got much worse recently.'

'He hasn't forgotten his birthday on Friday,' said Enid. 'He *never* forgets that. I want to give him the best present in the whole world.'

'The best present in the whole world would be a visit from his brother, King Wortle,' said the Queen. Once more Digory noticed the Queen and Enid grow sad at the mention of King Wortle's name.

'What's wrong?' Digory asked. 'Why don't we just invite him? It must be King Wortle's birthday too?'

'That *is* what's wrong,' said Enid. 'King Wortle disappeared from his home, Claggyboot Castle, on his birthday ten years ago and hasn't been seen since.'

'King Widget misses him so much,' said the Queen. 'They were best friends, you see, as well as brothers.'

Digory looked at his own best friend, Enid. He remembered how awful he felt when the dragon Horrible Gnasher Toast'em Firebreath wanted to gobble her up for breakfast. How unhappy he would be if she disappeared and was never seen again.

'We'll have to think of something very special for Daddy's birthday to cheer him up,' said Enid. 'Maybe a piglet race? He likes a nice squealy piglet race – the squeakier the better.'

Cook arrived with the roast parsnips.

'Have you seen the King?' asked the Queen.

'No, Your Majesty,' Cook replied. 'He didn't have any supper and he didn't have any breakfast and it doesn't look as if he wants any lunch, either!'

'That's unusual,' said the Queen. 'He must be feeling worse.' She put four of the crispiest, golden parsnips on the King's plate. 'I'll see if

I can tempt him myself.' And off she went to find him.

While the Queen was gone, Enid and Digory began to plan the piglet race.

'Let's give them a nice mud bath at the end,' said Digory.

'And tubs of turnips,' said Enid, 'and . . .'

Suddenly the Queen flew through the doorway, her wimple streaming and her face as white as milk.

'The King is gone!' she cried. '*He has disappeared!*'

Chapter Four

FORGETFULNESS

EVERYONE in the castle, from the black-smith to the dairymaid, hunted for King Widget. Digory searched the King's favourite snoozing places. Enid knew the secret haunts where her father liked to hide when the Queen had a list of things for him to do. But he wasn't to be found in any of them.

'No one saw him leave the castle,' sobbed the Queen. 'He just disappeared, like his brother – and with the sneezes!'

Enid comforted her mother. 'Maybe he left a clue somewhere.'

The Queen fetched the King's diary. 'This will tell us what was on his mind . . .'

King Widget liked to keep a diary. It helped him to remember things.

The Queen read it aloud:

'Monday.
   Ruled all day. Decided to organise a charge-and-thrust.
Tuesday.
   Ruled all day. Lost bedsocks.
Wednesday.
   Ruled all morning. Went for a walk. Found one of W's old chessmen in the juice-drippy-munch-place. Missed W.
Thursday.
   Took the day off. Forty winks under squeak-squeak-bang. Missed W.

Friday.
  Watched E and D play hoop-and-tortoise.
  Found bedsocks in cat's basket.
  P.S. Must visit W.'

'What does it all mean?' puzzled Digory.

'W . . .' said Enid. 'That must be Wortle.'

'And the juice-drippy-munch-place might be the orchard,' suggested Digory. 'But squeak-squeak-bang?' None of them could guess until they heard a familiar racket outside – the sound of the drawbridge being lowered. Each turn of the chain wheel made an excruciating squeak. Then it hit the ground with a loud thud and a 'cock-a-doodle-do' as the cockerel made off without his tail feathers.

'Aha,' muttered the Queen, '*that's* where he was when I wanted to visit Mother on Thursday.'

'Do you think he went to find King Wortle?' Digory wondered.

'It does look as though he forgot that his

brother disappeared,' said Enid. 'He must have gone off to Claggyboot Castle.'

'All by himself and with the sneezes!' gasped the Queen. 'Digory, dear, you are the prince. You must find him at once. And take him a clean handkerchief.'

Now, Digory had been asked to do many things he thought he couldn't (and been made to do some things he wished he hadn't), but he jumped up at once, like a true prince, to rescue the King.

'I'll find him, Your Majesty,' he said, secretly sliding a couple of roast parsnips into his pocket in case he wasn't back for tea. 'I promise. I won't return without him.'

'Then I'm coming too,' said Enid. 'I'll pack a picnic and saddle up my pony.'

Digory smiled gratefully and sneaked the parsnips back.

Before you could say 'royal rescue' Enid had saddled up her pony, Flibbertigibbet, and Barley too. Digory brought the picnic basket, the magic sword and a map to show them the way to Claggyboot Castle. And, with a reassuring wave to the Queen, they trotted over the drawbridge . . .

THE SOGGY SEARCH

Digory and Enid travelled along a river, through the greenwood, over a small hill, over a large hill and up a mountain path. Here, in unfamiliar territory, they stopped to look at the map.

Digory had had doings with maps before.

'Are you sure it's the right way up?' he asked Enid as she studied it closely.

'Yes,' said Enid. 'Look, there's "N" for north at the top.'

'But how do you know which way north is?' asked Digory.

'Because that's the way the map is pointing,' replied Enid confidently. Digory, very happy

to leave the directions to someone else, decided not to ask any further.

A wind shook the trees and the sky darkened.

I do hope the King has arrived somewhere, Digory thought, *wherever he has gone.*

'Look, here's Claggyboot Castle,' Enid pointed to a small inky picture of a tower, 'at the end of the valley on the other side of this mountain.' But, as Digory peered at the map, the tower mysteriously melted away before their eyes, leaving nothing but a blue smudge.

'Oh no, it's a magic map!' gasped Digory. 'Or else . . .' Cautiously he raised his head to see if there was a wizard leaning over their shoulders making mischief. Splat! A fat raindrop smacked him in the eye.

Enid hurriedly rolled up the parchment before the whole map was washed away and stuffed it inside her tunic. 'We'd better look for shelter,' she said.

Thunder rolled and the mountain echoed back with a growl. Black, grumpy clouds crowded the sky, looking for a big, wet fight.

Digory spotted a cave in the mountainside. 'That should be large enough for all of us.'

Suddenly a spear of lightning stabbed the sky. Flibbertigibbet took fright and reared up, tumbling Enid on to the grass. Then, with a whinny, the scatty pony bolted off down the path, taking the picnic with her!

At that moment the big, rainy cloud fight began. Digory, Enid and Barley made a dash for the cave.

'Are you hurt?' asked Digory.

'Oh no,' Enid grinned and rubbed her bruises, 'I'm used to that. But I do hope Daddy is out of the rain . . .'

Digory and Enid sat and watched the storm all afternoon. They played 'I spy' and sang songs to keep their spirits up. Barley settled herself at the back of the cave.

Presently an eerie rumble echoed around them. Enid stared nervously over her shoulder. She wondered if there was a tunnel in the darkness behind them. 'Do you think there are sleeping dragons in this mountain?' she whispered.

'I don't think so.' Digory blushed. 'That's my hunger-rumble!' But the picnic had galloped away — what could they eat? Digory wished he had kept those roast parsnips he'd smuggled into his pocket at lunch. He decided to try to brew up some soup.

Digory knew all about edible herbs and roots from his days spent rambling in the woods around Batty-by-Noodle. He gathered what he could find near the cave entrance and put them into his helmet, which he filled with rainwater. He also knew how to light a good fire, being the son of a blacksmith. However, even the best blacksmith needed dry sticks. Digory's were all wet.

'Why don't you try the magic sword?' suggested Enid. Digory heaped up the sticks and pointed the sword. Nothing happened. They waited. Nothing happened again. But this was the sort of magic sword it was – slow and not very enthusiastic. Then, like a glimmer of hope, a tiny speck of light began to glow, deep in the wet bundle. Slowly, it grew into a little red tongue that began to lick those sticks and to Digory and Enid's delight, there was soon a crackling fire and a helmet full of bubbling broth.

After their cheering meal of soup, followed by a handful of damp blackberries and hazel-nuts, Enid and Digory tried to use the sword to make the storm move along to the next mountain. But sadly, as they'd expected, the magic was not strong enough for that. The rainstorm continued on into the evening, until there was nothing for it but to stoke up the fire, make themselves comfortable and spend the night in the cave.

Things That Go Crack in the Night . . .

Digory had a happy dream that King Widget was sleeping in the same cave and they were all reunited in the morning.

Well, there was someone sleeping at the back of the cave that night – or at least some-*thing*.

As Enid had feared there *was* a tunnel in the darkness behind them. And at the other end of that tunnel, deep under the mountain, was a great cavern. And in that cavern, on a nest of bones, was a large egg. And in that egg

was something, fast asleep, waiting to be born . . .

In the middle of the night the egg started to crack. Out popped a tiny claw. Then another. Out peeped a tiny, green eye.

A little dragon pushed her horny head through the shell and looked about for her mother. But her mother wasn't there – she was twenty leagues away, chomping on a poor unfortunate maiden who'd been riding home at twilight, wearing very flashy jewels.

The baby dragon sniffed the air. A wisp of smoke drifted into the cavern from the mouth of a tunnel nearby.

Now, to a fire-breathing dragon a whiff of smoke is very comforting. She clambered out of the egg, stretched her trembling wings and shuddered. The cavern was cold and empty. So she set off along the tunnel towards the source of the smoke, hoping to find her mother . . .

Chapter Five

A Morning Surprise

B ARLEY opened one eye. A beam of morning light danced between her ears. So far so good.

But other things weren't quite right. She was not in her stable. She was not sitting on comfy straw. And something told her she was probably not going to get a nosebag of sweet hay for breakfast.

Something else was wrong. Nuzzled up beside her, with its head buried in her mane, was a small dragon. Barley opened the other eye.

The baby dragon, feeling the old carthorse stir, lifted its face to Barley's, blinked happily and licked her nose.

Barley had never had a foal of her own. Thinking about this arrangement for a moment, she decided it felt good. So she nestled her new baby closer and went back to sleep.

POUNCE

Enid woke Digory with the good news that the sun was shining. 'And look what I found in my pocket this morning,' she said. 'A bag of bramble jellybeans! They're a bit squashed but they'll make a good breakfast and then we must be on our way. Do you think Barley could carry us both?'

'D-d-d-' stuttered Digory.

'Are you cold?' asked Enid.

'D-d-d-' repeated Digory.

'Is it a game?' asked Enid. 'Something beginning with "d?" Can't we have breakfast first?'

'D-d-d-' Digory raised his shaking hand and pointed toward Barley.

'Oh! DRAGON!' squealed Enid.

Digory grabbed Enid's hand and pulled her out of the cave. They made a dive for the nearest bush and scrambled beneath it, out of sight.

Enid and Digory whispered fiercely under the bush.

'We have to wake up Barley!'

'How can we do that without waking up the dragon?'

'Do you think it's big enough to eat Barley?'

'No.'

'Do you think it's big enough to eat us?'

'No.'

'Do you think it's big enough to breathe fire?'

A sudden flicker of sparks at the back of the cave answered that question. The dragon's fiery sigh had set Barley's mane alight. Digory scrambled out from under the bush, ran into the cave, grabbed his helmet and threw the rest of the cold soup over Barley's head. Horse and dragon woke up with a start.

Enid peered out from under the bush in terror. Digory stood, frozen to the spot.

Barley shaking the soup from her ears,

staggered to her feet and ambled out into the sunshine. The little dragon followed.

Barley found a patch of long grass and began to help herself to breakfast. The little dragon watched for a moment and did the same.

Barley stamped her hoof and twitched her tail. So did the little dragon.

Then, as Digory and Enid watched in astonishment, Barley lay down and rolled in the warm grass and the little dragon tumbled playfully beside her.

'That dragon thinks Barley is her mother!' said Enid. And so she did.

Digory and Enid soon saw they were in no danger of being eaten by their new friend, but neither could they seperate the little dragon from her adopted mother.

'Well, either we leave Barley behind with the dragon and continue on foot,' Digory said to Enid, 'or we take her with us.'

There was really no choice. After a quick

look at the map Digory and Enid both climbed on to Barley's back and set off once more along the mountain path, with the little dragon tagging along behind.

The dragon was easily distracted by birds and butterflies and even by her own tail, which she leapt on whenever it swung into view. So they named her Pounce and everyone, especially proud Barley, was delighted with their new travelling companion.

Digory was also distracted by anything that flew into view – but for a different reason. He was worried that Pounce's real mother might return at any moment and mistake them for dragon-burglars . . .

On the King's Trail

Digory was relieved when, at last, they left the open mountain path and took a shady track along the edge of a forest. *At least we'll be able to dive into the wood if any trouble comes along*, he told himself. Still, he watched the sky warily. 'If only we had a disguise for Pounce,' he muttered.

At these words a brown cloak fell out of a branch above and landed on the little dragon's head. Pounce gave a snort of surprise and set fire to it.

In the sudden confusion a long stick and net also fell out of the tree, followed by a wide-brimmed hat and a plump, red-faced man, who clambered down after them, puffing and panting. He pulled the cloak off Pounce at once and stamped on the flames.

'Smouldering stitches!' he cried. 'You can't just go around setting fire to a fellow's cloak like that. I'll be all a-shiver this winter! Mrs Buzz will have to patch it up with bee fur.'

Mr Buzz, as you might guess, was a bee-keeper.

'Well, what were you doing up in that tree?' asked Digory.

'Looking for my bees,' he said. 'Though all

this fuss will have scared them off to Timbuktu!'

Enid looked closely at Mr Buzz's smoking cloak. Scarlet threads showed through here and there. Sure enough, it wasn't brown at all, but red cloth covered in mud. 'This is the King's cloak!' she cried excitedly.

'Poppycock!' said Mr Buzz. 'It's my very own.'

'My father, the King, has disappeared,' explained Enid. 'Prince Digory and I have come to look for him. This cloak may give us a clue.'

Mr Buzz sat down on his hat in disbelief. Digory and Enid hadn't noticed that after being caught in the rain and sleeping in a cave they didn't look like a prince and princess at all. 'How do I know you aren't clever cloak-thieves?' asked Mr Buzz suspiciously.

Digory, who was already feeling like a guilty dragon-burglar, thought this was very unfair. 'We don't want to steal anything,' he said. 'We want to find the King.' Suddenly he had an idea. 'Look inside the collar,' he said. 'The King always has the name of things sewn into his clothes.'

Sure enough, when Mr Buzz looked inside the collar, he found a label the Queen herself had stitched, saying 'Cloak'.

Mr Buzz looked very bashful. 'Your Majesties, Your Most Royal Highnesses.' He bowed to Enid and Digory. 'I never knew it was the King's cloak. I bought it yesterday from Truffle, the pig man,' he said. 'Paid him two honest shillings.'

'Then I'll give you two shillings for it,' said Enid, 'if you tell us how to find him.'

Mr Buzz told them the way through the wood to Truffle's cottage. 'You'll know when you're getting close . . .' he said mysteriously. 'And if you see my bees, just send them home.'

They set off through the wood and Digory wondered how he might explain to a swarm of bees that it was time to go home. He was still pondering the danger and difficulty of this when his nose suddenly told him that Truffle's cottage was near. As the pig-pong grew stronger they heard a scurry of little trotters among the bushes. They found Truffle emptying a sack of apples into his cart.

'Fine morning,' said Truffle shyly. He offered an apple to Barley but nearly jumped out of his skin when Pounce appeared from behind her, neighing hungrily. (She'd been quick to pick up Barley's voice as well as her habits.)

'Could you give her an apple too, please,' said Digory. 'She thinks she's a horse.'

Truffle stuck an apple on the end of a stick and offered it to Pounce at arm's length.

Enid saw how nervous he was and asked quickly about her father's cloak.

'I got it from Clod, the well-digger,' said Truffle. 'Paid him one honest shilling too.'

Digory thanked him and bought enough apples to fill their saddlebag. Then on they went to the village where Clod the well-digger lived.

To their dismay Clod the well-digger had no news about King Widget. 'I got it down the market, from Nell the stocking-maker,' he said. 'Paid her an honest sixpence.'

Digory and Enid tramped on to the market square.

Naughty Nell pretended she'd made the cloak herself. But when Enid showed her the label, Nell admitted she'd got it from Crust the baker.

They found Crust the baker who said he'd got it from Botch the carpenter.

They found Botch the carpenter, who said he'd got it from Slurp the slop-bucket boy.

They found Slurp, who wouldn't say a word about the cloak, until Digory warned him he had a magic sword – then Slurp burst into tears and said he stole it from Hop the innkeeper.

So Digory and Enid followed the King's trail to the edge of the village and a down-at-heel tavern called The No One Inn.

FUNNY LITTLE HABITS . . .

Clutching her father's burnt, muddy cloak, Enid went inside to find Hop the innkeeper, while Digory took Barley and Pounce round the back to the tavern stable for a drink of water.

As Digory waited for Enid, the delicious smell of rabbit stew wafted towards him from the cottage next door. *Maybe there's a little extra in the pot for a hungry prince*, thought Digory hopefully and he slipped off to find out.

While he was gone Barley spotted a nosebag of hay hanging at the back of the stable. *Maybe there's a little extra in the bag for a hungry horse*, she thought . . .

Just as Digory sat down at the kind neighbour's table for a bowl of stew a cry of panic rang out.

'FIRE! FIRE! THE STABLE'S ON FIRE!'

Digory leapt to his feet – it had to be Pounce! He ran to the tavern just in time to see a huge angry innkeeper, with muscles like pumpkins, run out with a pitchfork. 'Who set my stable alight?' Hop roared. 'I'll have his guts for garters!'

Digory looked around. A small, scorched, green tail was slithering into the wood.

'Hey, you there . . . suspicious stranger!' the innkeeper thundered. Digory decided it was not the moment to make friends. He dived into the wood and scrambled after Barley and Pounce as fast as his jelly legs would carry him.

ALL IS LOST!

Digory kept running through the bushes and brambles until he could no longer hear the innkeeper's shouts. Then he stopped to catch his breath. *Where was Enid? Why hadn't she come back?*

Pounce licked his nose, as if she knew she'd done something wrong. Her sooty breath made Digory feel very guilty. Through the trees he could see sparks flying from the burning stable. 'It's not your fault, Pounce.' He stroked her scaly forehead. 'I shouldn't have left you. And I shouldn't have run away.'

Although King Widget had never given Digory a list of things princes were supposed to do, Digory was certain that they *weren't* supposed to run away. Or at least, the good ones weren't. He felt very bad indeed. (But would *you* have risked a stab from Hop's pitchfork?) How could he make things right again? *I know — I'll try the magic sword*, he thought. *If the sword can* make *fire maybe it can put fire out. I could creep back to the stable secretly . . .*

He reached for the sword — but it wasn't hanging from his belt. He'd left it in the stable!

Poor Digory felt hopeless. Now the sword was lost, the King was lost and Enid was lost too! *Who or what will be next*? he thought.

As Digory wondered what to do he realised the answer to his own question — he was lost himself because Enid had the map!

Digory was flummoxed. He just didn't know what to do next. He pulled some apples out of the saddlebag and the three lost friends munched gloomily together. What chance was there now of finding the King? Digory had promised the Queen he wouldn't return without him. He wished with all his heart that Enid was there with one of her good ideas. Digory remembered her advice at the joust: Just pretend. *Maybe it was worth a try again*, he thought. So he shut his eyes and pretended she was right there beside him, eating an apple too.

'What should I do now?' asked Digory.

'Stick to our plan, and look for the King,' said the pretend Enid.

'But where shall I look?' asked Digory.

'At Claggyboot Castle,' said the pretend Enid, spitting out an apple pip.

'How will I find it without the map?' asked Digory.

'Ask that old man collecting acorns over there . . .' said the pretend Enid and, licking her juicy fingers, she disappeared.

Chapter Six

DIRECTIONS

THE old man collecting acorns directed Digory to a winding road that took him out of the woods and along the riverbank.

Digory was much happier. He felt Enid was with him somehow, although he had no real idea where she was. As always, her advice seemed right. *After all*, Digory told himself,

you can only rescue one person at a time.
Maybe Enid went off because she'd caught
sight of the King. Maybe they would both be
waiting for him at Claggyboot Castle . . .

As the day went on little Pounce, who was
still so new, began to feel tired and dawdled
behind. Barley kept waiting patiently for her
to catch up and eventually nudged her in
front, so she could give her an encouraging
nuzzle every now and then.

Digory looked out for signposts to the castle. There were plenty of milestones along the
way but not one of them mentioned
Claggyboot. They only marked the distance
back to the No One Inn or forward to
Warlock's Haunt – neither of which Digory
wanted to visit. Still, the acorn man had
seemed certain enough when he pointed in
that direction.

'I expect it's just around the next bend,'
Digory promised weary Pounce.

Well, of course it wasn't. Did you guess? However there was a little chapel with a Digory-length bench in the porch. It seemed the perfect place to rest. While Barley and Pounce nestled together on the grass nearby, Digory stretched out and had a nap.

If only he had gone *inside* he might have found someone familiar, also taking a rest . . .

Refreshed and keen to continue his search, Digory left the chapel and carried on along the road.

Five miles to Warlock's Haunt. On they went.

Four miles to Warlock's Haunt. On they went.

Three miles to Warlock's Haunt. When would they find a sign to Claggyboot? *If I'm having trouble finding it*, Digory wondered, *how did King Widget manage? Did the King even remember where he was going at all?*

Once more the little dragon grew tired. Digory found a shady bank beneath a bridge and they stopped for another rest.

If only Digory had rested *beside* the bridge he might have met someone familiar walking across . . .

Again they went on. A pie man came whistling down the lane. Digory always had a pie-shaped space inside, hoping to be filled.

'Three apple pies for my horse, please,' said Digory, 'two for my . . . er . . . other horse, and two for myself. One for now and one for later,' he added, not wanting to appear greedy.

The pie-man shook his head sadly. 'You just missed the last one, I'm afraid,' he said. 'Sold it to a young maiden.'

Digory sighed. Three tummies rumbled emptily.

'But you'll find plenty of food for your-self and your horses over the hill,' said the pie-man kindly. 'They're having a mudfling-ing match today.'

Digory thanked him. 'And have you seen a lost king wandering this way?' he asked.

'No, not this week,' said the pie-man, shaking his head. 'I've seen a runaway cartwheel, a dog with a string of sausages and a giant eagle. But, sorry, no kings.'

Digory tramped on over the hill and saw before him a castle surrounded by muddy fields. Not a pretty place to live but the perfect spot for a great clod-splattering, splurge-wallowing mudfling.

Sure enough the tournament had begun and a great crowd gathered to watch and cheer the teams. There were stalls selling toffee apples and barley twist, and a hog roast crackling on a spit.

With a giddy-up from Digory, Barley slipped and skidded down the hill and Pounce slid along behind her.

Pounce whinnied with excitement, setting

fire to a mud-smeared sign as she tumbled
past. Unnoticed, 'WARLOCK'S HAUNT –
KEEP OUT!' was reduced to a pile of cinders.

Chapter Seven

REUNITED!

AT the tournament Digory soon ate his fill of delicious treats. He was quite keen to hang around and watch a few fistfuls of the match, but he knew the Queen was desperately waiting for news of King Widget. 'I'm afraid there's no time to lose, old friend,' he said to Barley. 'We must find our way to

Claggyboot Castle.' Barley, already so mud-splattered that she looked like a dappled pony, didn't seem to object.

However, before he took a step Digory heard a familiar, spine-chilling sound.

'Aaaarahaieeeeee!'

'What teams are playing?' he asked a boy at the back of the crowd.

'It's the Filthy Wenches versus the Mucky Maidens,' said the boy.

The Mucky Maidens – his sister, Ethelburg's team! And if Digory was not mistaken that was her second-best war cry, only slightly less fierce than her Captain's rally.

'HHUUURGHARAAAAAAAAGH!!!'

That was the one. The crowd went wild. Digory climbed on to Barley to get a look. A twenty-armed, twenty-legged mud monster squirmed and struggled in the middle of the pitch. Digory could just make out the figure of Ethelburg drenched in a slurry of gloop. Then, to his amazement, he spotted Enid in the crowd opposite.

'Enid!' he shouted. But the cheering drowned his voice. Digory jumped down and tried to edge his way towards her through the excited throng, but it was impossible to push through. No matter how hard he tried he found himself shoved to the back, where he suddenly stopped in disbelief – for there he saw King Widget himself, standing on a milking stool, licking a toffee apple and watching the match!

OH HAPPY DAY!

Digory couldn't believe his eyes – the King safe, Enid found and Ethelburg thrilling the crowd!

'Make way, let me through,' he cried, 'I must get to the –'

SPLAT! A giant glob of mud spun over the heads of the cheering spectators and knocked poor Digory out.

Chapter Eight

WARLOCK'S HAUNT

WHEN Digory came to he was in a dim,
damp dungeon.

'Where am I?' he said. 'And *who* am I?'

Oh dear . . .

Sir Fearless

Digory had completely lost his memory.

He looked around in bewilderment. After some thought he decided there were only two things he could be sure of. First, he was definitely in a dungeon and second, he was definitely in trouble.

Digory examined his surroundings. Previous inhabitants had scratched messages on the walls such as '*I didn't do it, really*', and '*Home sweet home*'. Neither of these cheered him up much. There was one small, dirty broken window but it was too high to reach. The only sounds he could hear outside were cross geese and creaky cartwheels.

Maybe my clothes will tell me who I am, he thought. Digory rifled through his pockets, but they had been expertly picked by a scoundrel in the crowd at the mudflinging match and were quite empty. He studied his clothes. They looked as though they'd been

out in the rain, slept in and drenched with mud. *So*, he concluded, *I'm someone without a penny in the world, who sleeps in his clothes and lives in a muddy place. That doesn't sound like a good life.* He sighed. *Maybe I'm better off in a dungeon after all.*

Poor Digory. He couldn't even remember Enid's smiling face to lift his spirits.

For two days and nights Digory was kept in the dungeon, with nothing but a straw mattress and a brown mouse for company.

The only person he saw was an old man, who brought him food and drink. The dungeon keeper wasn't allowed to talk to Digory, in fact he seemed quite afraid of him and shuffled nervously away as soon as his duties were done.

On the third day Digory was brought before Sir Fearless, the Lord of the Castle. A crowd had gathered in the great hall.

'Where am I?' Digory said, blinking in the light. 'And, er . . . *who* am I?'

As he spoke everyone in the room hushed.

'He's lost his memory,' whispered a little boy.

'Ssh. It's only a trick,' hissed his father.

'You are a prisoner at Warlock's Haunt,' said Sir Fearless sternly. 'And we know you are a wizard!'

'A *wizard*!' Digory was amazed. He tried out this thought in his head but it didn't seem familiar. 'Are you sure?'

'We know you are a wizard because you travelled here with a dragon,' said Sir Fearless. 'And only wizards can tame dragons.'

'A *dragon*!' gasped Digory. 'Did I really?'

'Indeed,' said Sir Fearless. 'A small one,' he added.

'But why am I a prisoner?' asked Digory the Wizard.

'Long ago our King upset a powerful wizard, who came to this castle in disguise,' said Sir Fearless, 'so the wizard put a spell on him and made him disappear – right there, on that throne! No one has dared sit on it ever since.' He frowned. 'It was a sad day and a terrible nuisance. I am only his second-cousin-once-removed on his mother's side, but there was nobody else to rule the land.' Sir Fearless sighed deeply. 'Fishing is really my thing, you know,' he said. 'Anyway, since then wizards have been forbidden to come here. We changed the name of the castle to put them off, but it obviously hasn't worked.'

Digory felt sorry for Sir Fearless. Somewhere, in the back of his mind, he did remember fishing, and it seemed a happy thought.

'If I *am* a wizard,' he said, 'maybe I can think of a spell to bring your king back again?'

Sir Fearless considered this. 'How do I know I can trust you?' he said. 'You might turn me into a newt?'

Digory could see his point of view. *How could he even trust himself*, he wondered.

'No,' said Sir Fearless with a heavy heart.

'You're quite small for a wizard and don't seem much trouble, but I can't see what else to do except have your head chopped off.'

Chapter Nine

DIGORY IN DANGER

BEFORE Digory had a chance to protest, faint or run away, the old dungeon keeper came running into the great hall crying, 'FIRE, FIRE, THE STABLE'S ON FIRE!'

'It's that dragon!' groaned Sir Fearless. 'Take the wizard back to the dungeon.

Everyone else, grab a bucket and follow me to the well. I'll have *both* their heads chopped off tomorrow. What I'd give for a quiet day's fishing!'

Back in his dungeon Digory, believing himself to be a wizard, tried some spells to get himself out of trouble. As he was used to composing songs and poems, Digory found he could make up spells quite easily.

'Change my size and change my shape –
Through this keyhole I'll escape!

Cold as ice and hot as mustard,
Turn these stone walls into custard!

Down the well all axes drop,
Save this wizard from the chop!'

The spells were not very good (but then neither were his poems). And none of them worked.

'Something's missing . . .' pondered Digory. That something, of course, was a wizard.

It seemed that Digory was destined for the chop in the morning. He rattled his well-locked door and searched for a loose stone or secret tunnel in the dungeon, but there was no escape.

Once more he was left with the last, unlikely hope that he'd wake up and find it had all been a bad dream.

Digory did wake up in the middle of the night, but he was still in the dungeon. Something hard and heavy had been pushed through the window and hit him on the head.

'Oddsboddikins!' he cried, jumping up. 'What was that? What am I doing here?' The well-aimed blow had not just given him a bump – it had given him his memory back!

For a long while Digory sat and thought about everything that had happened since he'd arrived at the mudflinging match. Like a jigsaw with missing pieces he could patch together some of it, but the whole picture wasn't clear. Some things just didn't make sense.

Digory felt around for what had hit him. In the darkness he cut his finger on the blade of a sword. Why, that could have killed him with one blow! He looked up at the high dungeon window. Who could have tried to kill him in the night? *They really don't like wizards around here at all*, he thought.

Still, a sword would be useful in getting out of his predicament. Digory picked it up. Tied around the handle was a note. He held it up to a thin shaft of moonlight and read the message on it.

Dear Digory,
Use this to get yourself out of trouble,
then meet me on the drawbridge

Enid x

Enid was there, at the castle! So it was the
magic sword! Digory's spirits rose.

At once he pointed the sword at the dungeon door. After the usual delay it swung
open with a creak. Digory rushed out and
promptly fell on his face.

'Ouch!' he cried.

'Ouch!' cried the bundle of rags he had
tripped over. It was the dungeon keeper, trying to get some sleep. With great apologies,
Digory took the torch from the wall and
helped the old man to his feet. Then his
mouth dropped open – for that old man
dressed in rags was none other than King
Widget himself!

'Your Majesty!' gasped Digory.

'Ah yes!' said the King, sitting on the stone

step. 'Thought you looked familiar, Diggers old boy. Not the wizard type at all. Still, you can't be too careful with chaps disappearing and all that!'

Digory used his sword once more to provide the King with a new set of warm, dry clothes and, as the Queen had insisted, a clean hand-kerchief.

'How did you come to be in this dreadful place, Sire?' asked Digory. 'The Queen was so worried when she couldn't find you.'

'Silly old fruit,' chuckled the King. 'Nothing to worry about. Just a bit of dungeon work – does a man good to do an honest day's work now and then. Mind you, I do miss the royal, um, you know . . . plumpy-feathersome-spring 'n' bounce?'

'You miss your bed!' laughed Digory.

'Yes.' The King laughed too. 'A fellow gets a bit stiff sleeping on the floor. Not so young as I used to be, eh!'

Digory asked the King how he had come to be a dungeon keeper. The King explained, in his forgetful, muddled way, that he had gone up to the battlements at Widget Castle to watch the joust when a great giant eagle had swooped down and carried him off.

'Took me for miles in its enormous grab-bers,' the King said, wide-eyed.

'Claws,' said Digory.

'Exactly,' said the King. 'My shiny ring-a-ding fell off . . .'

(*Crown*, guessed Digory.)

'My red roundabout fell off.'

(*Cloak*, guessed Digory.)

'Then I fell off, too. Bit of a drop, Diggers, but the fresh air did wonders for my sneezes and I landed in, you know, yucky mucky goo.'

'Mud, Your Majesty!'

'That's it. Then it began to pitter-patter,' continued the King. 'Along came Sir Scare-em-off, riding back from his . . . oh . . . chase-the-antlers, and he brought me here to his castle.'

'Why didn't he send for us to take you home?' said Digory.

'Well, you know my little problem, lad,' said the King shyly. 'Couldn't tell him where I came from or who I was. Couldn't remember that word . . .'

'King!' said Digory.

'That's the one. Must have it stitched on to my . . . um . . . arms up, tuck your tail in.'

'Shirt.'

'Yes,' said King Widget. 'Sharp thinking.'

It seemed, however, that Sir Fearless had taken pity on the King and given him a hot meal and a job.

Now Digory told the King his news. 'Enid is here, Your Majesty, waiting at the draw-bridge.'

'Dear girl!' exclaimed the King. 'Let's go at once.'

But Digory persuaded the King to take a little detour on their way . . .

Chapter Ten

A LITTLE DETOUR . . .

As Digory and the King made their way silently through the courtyards and passages Digory pondered further on what had happened.

Didn't a King disappear at Warlock's Haunt some time ago?

Didn't somebody say they'd changed the name of the castle?

They came to the great hall. Digory stood before the throne.

'Hurry up, Diggers,' said King Widget impatiently, 'poor Enid's waiting on the up-and-over.'

'I think somebody else is waiting for you too, Your Majesty,' said Digory. He crossed his fingers for good luck and pointed the magic sword at the throne. Nothing. A bat fluttered in the rafters above. More nothing. *Maybe this needs wizard-strength magic?* thought Digory with disappointment.

Then, with a pop, as if he'd squeezed through a small invisible space, a royal figure appeared on the throne.

'Where's that tricky wizard?' said King Wortle, looking around. 'Where did he go?'

'Wortle!' cried King Widget in astonishment. 'Welcome back!' He threw his arms around his twin brother with delight.

King Wortle was completely baffled but happy indeed to see him.

'Where have you been all this time, eh?' asked King Widget. 'You disappeared ten years ago.'

King Wortle looked even more bamboozled. 'Well, I don't know where I've been,' he said, taking off his crown to scratch his head. 'I've quite forgotten.'

'Oh, don't worry, Worty,' King Widget reassured him, 'I forget things all the time. That's no problem, no problem at all.'

Digory smiled to himself. It seemed that the twin brothers had much more than their identical looks in common.

There followed a whole confusion of explanation about wizards and rescues and mud and dungeons, with lots of laughter and misunderstanding. Digory explained how Sir Fearless had reluctantly ruled since King Wortle disappeared.

'*Sir Fearless*, you say?' muttered King Wortle. 'I'm sure I don't have a relation with that name.'

At that moment Sir Fearless, woken up by

all the noise, appeared in his nightshirt.'

'Your Majesty!' he cried in astonishment.

'Herbert!' said the King.

It seemed that not only had the King's second-cousin-once-removed changed the name of the castle to frighten off wizards – he'd changed his own name too.

Herbert was delighted to learn that his ruling days were over, but as long as he lived he never understood how a dungeon keeper became a king and a wizard became a prince.

Herbert was not the only one woken up by the celebration. One by one, the other inhabitants of the castle staggered in, yawning and complaining about the noise. However, before you could say, 'Long live the King' they were all clapping and cheering and dancing in their slippers around the throne.

Now Enid, sitting alone on the drawbridge, heard the rumpus and riot too. She crept

across the dark courtyard, curious to see
what was going on . . .

'Ouch!'

'Ouch!'

'Who's that?'

'It's me!'

Enid tweaked a long, chipolata nose.
'Digory!' He had come to find her. They
hugged each other.

'But what's all that noise?' asked Enid.

'Come and see . . .'

Enid couldn't believe her eyes. A jubilant
crowd of people in their nightshirts were
cavorting in the great hall and in the middle
was her father, King Widget, skipping like a
schoolboy with his long-lost brother, Wortle!

What a reunion! Everything was explained
all over again, with even more confusion and
laughter. Enid added her story too. She told
everyone how she'd lost Digory at the No
One Inn because the bad-tempered innkeeper
had spilt cider on her dress. By the time she'd
mopped it dry the stable had caught fire and

Digory was nowhere to be seen. And she told them how she'd found the magic sword and made her own way to Warlock's Haunt by mistake, just like Digory.

'I always knew you weren't far away,' said Digory.

The party went on until dawn. When nobody could dance another step they raided the kitchen for a royal breakfast.

But at last Enid decided it was time to leave. 'Mummy will be so pleased to see you,' she reminded King Widget as he wiped the egg from his whiskers.

And it really did seem time to go home for a happy ending . . .

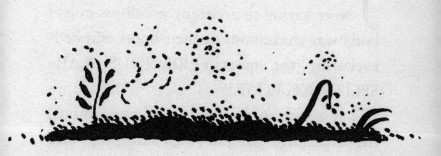

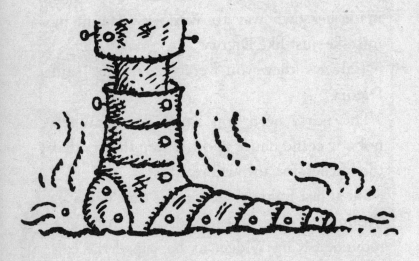

Chapter Eleven

ALMOST

JUST as Enid, Digory and King Widget were saying their sleepy goodbyes everybody was shaken out of their boots and bedsocks by the most FEROCIOUS, EAR-SPLITTING ROAR!!

They all ran to the windows. An enormous, fire-breathing dragon was stamping and

snorting flames on the other side of the moat.

The whole castle shook with panic.

Up went the drawbridge.

Out ran the archers, with their napkins still tucked into their nightshirts.

On to the fire went big cauldrons of oil.

Anyone who had armour put it on.

Anyone who didn't grabbed a saucepan to put on his head.

Anyone without a saucepan hid under the bed.

Everybody panicked – except King Widget.

'Don't worry, Wortle,' he said. 'It's just a dragon. Digory can deal with those – no trouble at all. Done it a hundred times, haven't you, lad?' And he sat back down and helped himself to another buttered crumpet.

No Trouble at All?

Digory stared out of the window at the dragon. He gulped and shuddered. Although he

had once been called Digory the Dragon
Slayer this was a name he'd acquired by mistake. He *had* once faced a dragon, it was true,
but it turned out to have no teeth. Whereas
this one had razor teeth and vicious claws
and monstrous horns and frazzling flames
and a very unfriendly look in its eye. Digory
turned around for encouragement and sup-
port, but apart from King Widget having his
second breakfast there was no one to be seen.
Even Enid was sitting under the table with a
pudding bowl on her head. Digory clutched

the magic sword. Maybe this time there wouldn't be a happy ending after all . . .

ANOTHER REUNION?

The drawbridge was lowered and Prince Digory stepped forward to face the dragon. Once more in his desperate hour he remembered Enid's advice – just pretend. *But what should I pretend this time*, he wondered miserably. The dragon reared up and snarled, shooting a jet of flame high into the sky. Digory decided to pretend to be invisible . . .

Meanwhile Barley hadn't stirred. Being deaf she hadn't heard the midnight party or the roaring dragon. And as Barley hadn't stirred, Pounce hadn't stirred either. But now the smell of the dragon's fiery breath reached her nose. Pounce sniffed. The smoke smelt delicious . . .

As Digory took a step on to the drawbridge

Pounce crept up shyly beside him, followed by Barley, who wasn't going to let her little one out of sight.

'That dragon's come for her baby,' whispered a stable boy. The whisper went round the castle and, although he couldn't hear it, Digory was thinking the very same thought himself.

Barley looked up at the big dragon. Her four knackety knees began to knock in terror. She looked at Pounce, cowering now beside her. Then she looked at Digory.

Digory nodded sadly and Barley understood. She snuffled and licked her little one for the last time. Then, putting a brave hoof forward, she gently nudged Pounce on to the drawbridge. Everybody held their breath . . .

The big dragon peered down at Pounce, trembling like a kitten. Slowly Digory began to step backwards. He gestured to Barley to do the same, but, whether out of fear or love, the old carthorse wouldn't budge. Suddenly the big dragon curled its lip and snarled. With

a terrified whinny, Pounce turned tail and scuttled back to Barley.

Everybody gasped!

Now it was Barley's turn to snort and stamp her hoof as if to say, 'What sort of mother does that?' Once more she pushed Pounce gently with her nose on to the draw-bridge.

Once more everybody at Claggyboot Castle held their breath . . .

Pounce looked back, but Barley nodded her on. Nervously she stepped forward and gazed up into the glowering green eyes of the big dragon. For a moment she seemed mes-merised . . . but then she shook an invisible mane, turned tail and scooted back to Barley.

'We're doomed!' everyone cried. 'We'll all be fried and gobbled!'

'WHAT'S THE MEANING OF THIS?' the big dragon roared.

Everyone looked at Digory. Pretending to be invisible had definitely not worked. 'It's not our f-f-fault,' he stuttered. 'We didn't steal her. She followed us. She thinks my h-h-horse is her m-m-mother . . .'

'I DON'T CARE ABOUT THAT!' bellowed the dragon. 'IT'S NOTHING TO DO WITH ME!'

'Haven't you come for your baby?' asked Digory.

'DO I LOOK THE MOTHERLY TYPE?' the dragon sneered. 'I'VE COME FOR TREASURE AND ALL YOUR JUICY MAIDENS. AND I'LL ROAST YOUR SCRAWNY RIBS TOO FOR GETTING IN MY WAY!'

At these loud and very clear words Barley pushed Pounce smartly into the moat and jumped in after her!

Digory was left to face the dragon alone.

WHO'S CHICKEN?

Digory didn't need to pinch himself – he wasn't going to wake up from a dream. He knew

116

there was no help to call on. He knew pretending wasn't going to work.

Then a voice from the castle shouted, 'Come on, Diggers, do what you dragon slayers do. Time to get back to the grand-gigglywimple.'

Even at that dreadful moment a smile crept on Digory's face. King Widget believed he was a dragon slayer. King Widget had made him a prince. And although Digory didn't know what princes were supposed to do, he was certain they had to protect their kings.

Digory took a deep breath. He stepped forward, drew his sword and pointed it at the dragon.

'I am Prince Digory, the Dragon Slayer. Be gone!' he cried.

The dragon stared in astonishment, then threw back her head and laughed, a deep, thunderous, dragon-belly laugh that shook the ground beneath Digory's feet and made the drawbridge rattle.

'I'M NOT AFRAID OF A SQUIRMY

WORM LIKE YOU!' she roared. 'I'LL TEAR THE STRINGY FLESH FROM YOUR SPINDLY BONES, I'LL . . . EURGH! . . . Awk! . . . chuck, chuck, chuck!'

With an explosion of scales and feathers the dragon turned into a chicken.

'HURRAY!' The castle echoed with cheers of relief. 'HURRAY FOR PRINCE DIGORY THE DRAGON SLAYER!'

Now it was Digory's turn to laugh as the dragon-chicken ran around in silly circles, squawking and snorting tiny puffs of black smoke from her beak. At the sound of her squawk the cockerel strutted up, and before you could say, 'how-d'ye-cock-a-doodle-do' that dragon-chicken ran off like the wind.

Barley and Pounce clambered, dripping, out of the moat.

'You're a good mother, Barley,' said Digory, patting her mane. 'When my hands have stopped shaking I'll find you both a carrot.' But in an instant Enid was there, with carrots and kisses and two happy kings.

'Well done, Diggers,' said King Widget. 'Funny foal you've got there – breed 'em with wings, eh? Young chaps these days,' he chuckled, 'full of new ideas.'

'Thank you, Digory,' said King Wortle, 'from myself and all my kingdom. You deserve a great reward.'

Digory shook his head bashfully. At that very moment he felt rewarded enough just being ungobbled. But King Wortle insisted on giving him the title of Royal Wizard of Claggyboot – and there was nothing Digory could say to change his mind.

THE UNFORGETTABLE DAY

'Now,' said King Widget with a twinkle in his eye, 'what day is it today?'

'It's our birthday!' cried King Wortle, who never forgot it either.

'Then I suggest we all go home to my um, you know . . . turrets-and-twirly-steps . . .'

'Castle,' giggled Enid.

'On the tip of my tongue,' said King Widget with a wink. 'And we'll have a great birthday knees-up-and-hurdy-gurdy! Better still, we'll have a charge and thrust! Yes, a great birthday charge and thrust. Everyone is invited. Diggers can do the jousting. No problem for a chap like him. Done it all before.'

Enid looked at Prince Digory the Dragon

Slayer, Royal Wizard of Claggyboot, whose heart had just sunk into his cold, tin boots. She tugged a lock of his ginger hair and grinned. 'Don't worry,' she whispered, 'I'm sure a piglet race will do just as well!'

Digory smiled with relief. 'Are you sure?'

Enid nodded.

'Then let's go home,' said Digory. After all, it really *was* time for a happy ending . . .

A Note on the Author

Angela McAllister is the author of over fifty books for children, several of which she has illustrated herself. Angela has two children who are fantastic bookworms and a brilliant inspiration. She lives with her family in a crumbly 16th Century cottage with an unruly garden on the edge of Cranborne Chase. This is Angela's eighth book for Bloomsbury.

A NOTE ON THE ILLUSTRATOR

Ian Beck is the author and illustrator of several books for children. He is well known for illustrating many wonderful and familiar nursery rhymes as well as winning gold with three of his books in the Right Start Best Toy Awards. He lives in London with his wife and children. This is Ian's third book for Bloomsbury.

By the same author and illustrator

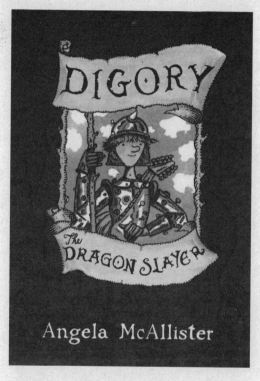

'Entertainingly topsy-turvy'
Guardian

'This funny fairy tale zips
along nicely'
Junior Education